Clifford
The SMALL
RED PUPPY

Story and pictures by Norman Bridwell

Scholastic Inc.

New York Toronto London Auckland Sydney
Mexico City New Delhi Hong Kong Buenos Aires

To Amy, Melissa, Beth, and Debbie

ISBN-13: 978-0-590-44294-7
ISBN-10: 0-590-44294-5

56 55 54 53 52   9 10 11 12/0
                          Printed in the U.S.A.   23

Hi! I'm Emily Elizabeth
and this is Clifford, my big red dog.

Yesterday my friend Martha said,
"I got my dog from a fancy pet store.
Where did you get yours?"

So I told her how I got Clifford.

When I was little I lived in the city.
I didn't have a dog.

One day the man down the hall called us.
His dog had puppies. He wanted to give me one.

One puppy was smaller than the rest.

The man said, "Don't take him. He is the runt.
He will always be small and sick."
But I loved that little puppy. He needed me.

I named my puppy Clifford.
He was so tiny that I had to feed him
with the doll's baby bottle.

We got the smallest collar we could find
for Clifford.

It was too big.

When he began to eat dog food,
we had to watch him all the time.

He was so little that he was always getting lost,
even in our small apartment.

Daddy said Clifford was just too small.
He didn't think he could live through the winter.
I was very sad.

That night I told Clifford I wished he would grow to be
a big healthy dog. I told him I loved him.

Next morning he looked bigger to me.

He seemed to have an easier time
eating his dog food.

And his collar wasn't so loose.

In fact, by the time Daddy got home
the collar was too small.

By bedtime Clifford's tiny basket
seemed a little too small for him.

So I let him sleep on my pillow again.

That was a mistake.

Next morning Mommy thought
Clifford looked different.
Daddy said, "I think he is growing."

I decided to take Clifford for a walk.
At the corner I saw a big dog coming.
I knew I should pick Clifford up
so the big dog couldn't hurt him.

I shouldn't have worried.

Clifford really was growing!
We ran home to show Mommy how big he was.

Had our apartment door grown smaller?

Daddy couldn't believe it. We put Clifford
in the garden to sleep that night.

In the morning the lady upstairs called us.
It was about Clifford.

In fact, all the neighbors
were starting to notice him.

The landlord called the police.
They came to see Clifford.
They said Clifford would have to go.
But how? He couldn't go through the door.

There was just one way to get him
out of our garden.

We sent him to live with my uncle
who lived in the country.

I was sad. I missed my little puppy.

And he missed me.

One day we got a surprise.
My uncle wanted Daddy to come work
with him in the country.
We moved right away.

Clifford was waiting for me.
I said, "Clifford, stop growing.
You are just right."

"So," I said to Martha,
"that's how I got my dog.
Tell me again how you got your dog."

Martha said, "Forget it."